Contents

Four-Legged Guide

Furry paws pad down the sidewalk next to a pair of human feet. But it isn't time for fun and games. This is a guide dog at work.

The owner holds onto the dog's **harness**, walking directly beside the four-legged guide. Both dog and owner stop at the curb. The team waits as cars speed by. When the zooming traffic stops, they cross the street safely.

Guide dogs lead people who are blind or who have **vision** loss.

Heroic Dogs

GUIDE DOGS

by Dale Jones

Consultant: Karen Shirk, CEO, 4 Paws for Ability

BEARPORT PUBLISHING

Minneapolis, Minnesota

Photo credits: Cover, ©Eric Isselee/Shutterstock; 3, ©Kasefoto/Shutterstock; 4, ©treasure dragon/Shutterstock; 5, ©Michael de Nysschen/Shutterstock; 6, ©alvarez/Getty Images; 7, ©Jim Craigmyle/Getty Images; 8, ©Eric Isselee/Shutterstock; 9, ©Jim Craigmyle/Getty Images; 10, © TwentySeven/iStock; 11, ©LWA/Getty Images; 12, ©Debbie Noda/Modesto Bee/ZUMAPRESS.com/Alamy; 13, ©Africa Studio/Shutterstock; 14, ©Scott Eisen/Getty Images; 15, ©Roman Chazov/Shutterstock; 16, ©BRIAN MITCHELL/Getty Images; 17, ©TPG/Getty Images; 18, ©otsphoto/Shutterstock; 19, ©hedgehog94/Shutterstock; 20, ©Altrendo Images/Shutterstock; 21, ©wavebreakmedia/Shutterstock; 22, ©Tibrina Hobson/Getty Images; 23, ©Dora Zett/Shutterstock

President: Jen Jenson
Director of Product Development: Spencer Brinker
Senior Editor: Allison Juda
Associate Editor: Charly Haley
Designer: Colin O'Dea

Library of Congress Cataloging-in-Publication Data

Names: Jones, Dale, 1990- author.
Title: Guide dogs / Dale Jones.
Description: Minneapolis : Bearport Publishing Company, 2021. | Series: Heroic dogs | Includes bibliographical references and index.
Identifiers: LCCN 2021001092 (print) | LCCN 2021001093 (ebook) | ISBN 9781636911151 (library binding) | ISBN 9781636911243 (paperback) | ISBN 9781636911335 (ebook)
Subjects: LCSH: Guide dogs--Juvenile literature.
Classification: LCC HV1780 .J66 2021 (print) | LCC HV1780 (ebook) | DDC 362.4/183--dc23
LC record available at https://lccn.loc.gov/2021001092
LC ebook record available at https://lccn.loc.gov/2021001093

For more information, write to Bearport Publishing, 5357 Penn Avenue South, Minneapolis, MN 55419. Printed in the United States of America.

Guide dogs always walk slightly ahead of their owners and usually stay on the left side.

A Second Set of Eyes

Guide dogs have important jobs. These furry workers are trained to help people who are blind avoid **obstacles** in daily life. The dogs allow their **handlers** to be more **independent** by acting as a second set of eyes. Don't pet or play with guide dogs if you see them. These working animals need to stay focused!

Some experts think dogs first started guiding people more than 2,000 years ago.

Guide dogs halt or sit to let their handler know there is a curb ahead. Then, both dog and owner cross when the owner decides it's safe.

The Perfect Pups

Which dogs make the best guides? Picking the perfect pups starts with choosing the right **breeds**. Labrador retrievers, German shepherds, and golden retrievers are all common breeds used as guide dogs. These animals are usually smart, easy to train, and make good **companions** to their human handlers. Guide dogs must also have a good memory, be quick learners, and be able to stay calm.

Every animal is different. Dogs that act nervous or aggressive around people or other animals can't be guide dogs.

German shepherds have been used as guide dogs for longer than any other breed.

A Family Start

Learning for guide dogs begins when the puppies are about two months old. Carefully chosen **foster families** raise the future working dogs for about a year. These families make sure the puppies are well cared for and that they learn to sit, stay, and walk on a leash. The dogs also learn to behave well and be **confident** in all kinds of situations.

The puppies go everywhere with their foster families. They have to get used to many different places, including stores, offices, and even airplanes.

Any family can be a foster family, as long as they are willing to teach and care for the dog.

Training Time

After fun with foster families, it's time for special training! When they are about 14 to 16 months old, guide dogs start their official training. The dogs learn to wear a harness and obey **cues**. Trainers teach them to start, stop, and turn left or right. The guide dogs are often taken to sidewalks and roads where they learn to look for possible dangers that their future handlers won't see.

When they are in training, guide dogs may live at training schools or at home with trainers.

Sometimes, guide dogs are trained to find specific things, such as escalators, doors, or mailboxes.

A Perfect Match

Once the dogs have completed their training, they're ready to be paired with human partners. Trainers carefully match guide dogs with handlers based on needs and personality. It's important to find a good fit since the dogs and their owners will work closely as a team. For example, a dog with a lot of energy may be matched with a very active person.

Guide dogs go everywhere with their owners. If its owner is a runner, a guide dog will need to go on runs, too.

In the United States, there are more than 10,000 teams of guide dogs and handlers.

The Team Together

After a match, the new handler trains with the guide dog. The team spends a few weeks learning together. The dog gets used to its handler, and the handler learns cues and then practices using them with their **canine**. When both dog and human are ready, the handler takes the guide dog home.

Training together also helps the guide dog and handler learn to trust each other.

A handler and guide dog may practice avoiding obstacles together.

Building a New Life

At home, dog and handler settle into their new life as a team. The dog learns the people and places that will be a part of its everyday working life. But life for a guide dog isn't all about work! Just like pet dogs, guide dogs need lots of play time and love. But when the harness goes on, the dog knows it's time for play to stop and work to begin.

Playing together can strengthen the bond between a handler and their guide dog.

If you see a dog with a vest on, that means the dog is on the job! Many guide dogs wear vests when they are working in public.

A Job Well Done

A guide dog usually works with its handler for about 8 to 10 years. Then, it's time for the hardworking dog to **retire**. Some guide dogs will continue to live with their handlers but will no longer work. Others will be adopted by families who will love and take care of them for the rest of their lives.

Because of the strong bond that these incredible animals have with their handlers, each guide dog will work with only one human during its lifetime.

Guide dog training programs find homes for retired guide dogs. There are often waiting lists for people who want to adopt one.

Meet a Real Guide Dog

Poppet met her handler Janet in February 2017. Now, the two spend every day together as they live and work in Oakland, California. Poppet guides Janet when they go out. "We are a team," Janet says. "She trusts me, and I trust her." When they are home, Janet often sits on the couch to watch TV with Poppet resting her chin on Janet's leg. "She keeps me safe 24/7," Janet says.

Poppet and Janet's story was shared in the movie *Pick of the **Litter***.

Poppet and Janet *(center)* pose with the directors of the movie.

Glossary

breeds groups of dogs that look and act in a similar way

canine a dog

companions animals or people who spend time together

confident having a feeling or belief that you can do something well or succeed at something

cues words or actions that signal a dog to do something

foster families families that take care of children or animals until they can find a forever home

handlers people who are led by guide dogs

harness a strap with a handle worn by a dog that its owner can hold

independent able to do things without help

litter a group of baby animals, such as puppies, that are born to the same mother at the same time

obstacles things that block a path

retire to stop working, usually because of age

vision the act or power of seeing

Index

Read More

Jones, Dale. *Service Dogs (Heroic Dogs).* Minneapolis: Bearport Publishing, 2022.

Laughlin, Kara L. *Guide Dogs (Dogs with Jobs).* New York: AV2 by Weigl, 2019.

Learn More Online

1. Go to **www.factsurfer.com**
2. Enter "**Guide Dogs**" into the search box.
3. Click on the cover of this book to see a list of websites.

About the Author

Dale Jones lives in Los Angeles, California, with his family and two dogs.